No one really believed in the folklore tale about the Greenwell Smoozles . . .

Or did they?

Deep inside the Greenwell cave,
A friendship had begun,
The Smoozle and the black cat,
Were now ready for some fun.

Tip-pawing back to Jolly Farmer Ed and Jo,
Tiddles crept back through the door.
Snuggled into her pussycat bed,
To join the choruses of snores . . .

Down at Greenwell cottage, curled up in her comfy bed,

This cat had many adventures, swimming around her head.

For Tiddles was really excited to see the Smoozle once again,

But the only question on her mind was how to escape and when.

The naughty dogs were waiting,
and chased her round the house.

But they were soon distracted,
by Magnus, the cottage mouse.

Through the dog flap she
tip-pawed, and headed
towards the shore,

And there the
Smoozle was waiting
beside the peedie
wooden door.

SMILE!

Hello Beyla!

Hroo Tiddles!

Hello Beyla Smoozle!

Hroo Tiddles Farm Cat!

Hello Beyla Smoozle of Greenwell!

Hroo Tiddles Farm Cat of Greenwell!

Down by the edge of Greenwell's stony well,

The pair stood silent, amongst the bluest of bluebells.

"Shall we go now?" Beyla smiled her toothy grin,

Tiddles meowed readily, **"Let, our adventures now begin!"**

The pair both took a strong deep breath, and closed their eyes quite tight,

Then jumped into the magic well, for a spiraling downward flight.

The colours flashed in clouds of light, that danced and twirled around,

Whooshes, whistles and trills whizzed by 'til their bottoms bumped the ground.

Down through the heather, far across the Hillside field,

Was a tiny little object, that scuttled around then kneeled.

The pair looked worried . . .

What could it be, and should we both beware?

Let's tip-paw a little closer, and peep to see what's there!

Down at Heather Hill, sitting on a grassy mound,
Was a teeny tiny vole, making a funny muttering sound.
"Oh bother, oh crumbs, I cannot see,
My eye blinks have gone away without me!"

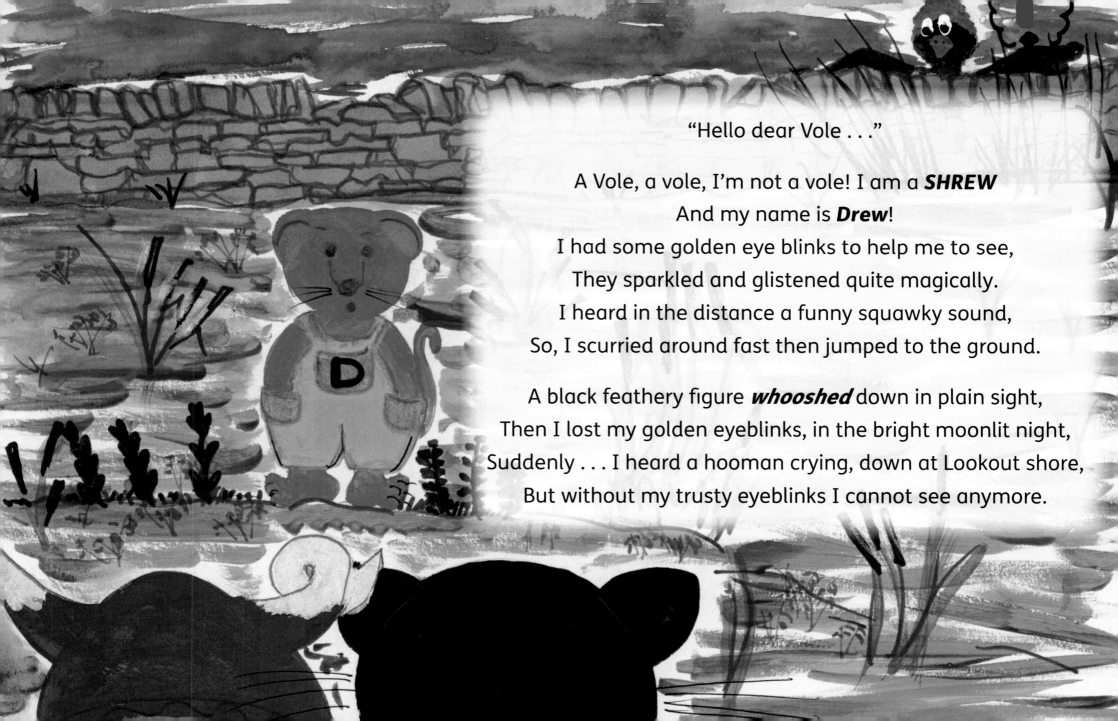

"Hello dear Vole . . ."

A Vole, a vole, I'm not a vole! I am a **SHREW**
And my name is **Drew**!
I had some golden eye blinks to help me to see,
They sparkled and glistened quite magically.
I heard in the distance a funny squawky sound,
So, I scurried around fast then jumped to the ground.

A black feathery figure **whooshed** down in plain sight,
Then I lost my golden eyeblinks, in the bright moonlit night,
Suddenly . . . I heard a hooman crying, down at Lookout shore,
But without my trusty eyeblinks I cannot see anymore.

Oh Drew . . . your eyeblinks . . .
We've looked around but really cannot find,
And awful crying fills the air, from that hooman kind.
So, let's all go to Lookout shore and we will surely see,
If that hooman can help us solve, The Eye Blink Mystery!

Down on Lookout shore,
the hooman cried and cried,

For around her tiny ankles were
clear tangles, tightly tied.

The three looked shocked . . .

**What could they do?
Should they go and help?**

When suddenly down on the rock
came a roaring yelp!

I am Sigrid Selkie, **No hooman am I!**

I live in the water but can also be dry,

My friend Sigurd helped me to swim to this shore,

For I could not swim, all alone anymore . . .

My tail fins all tangled in this clear funny stuff,

So, I came to this shore to untangle,
but it's tough!

I took hooman form instead of selkie paws,

As my tiny fingers are better than claws.

I laid out my coat in the bright moonlit night,

Then a black feathery figure
whooshed down in plain sight.

It looked straight at me with a twinkle in its eye,

Then it picked up my coat and flew right on by!

Oh, **please** can you all, help, untangle me,
Then find my selkie coat
or no return *to...*

the...

sea...

Beyla was sad and said hoomans DON'T CARE!
As plastic tangles can be seen **EVERYWHERE**.

All sizes, shapes and colours, they're scattered around,
Hiding in many places, hoping not to be found.

Tangles hurt so many creatures, so hear what we say,
**"Hoomans, we DON'T WANT your tangles,
please take them away!"**

But the selkie just wanted to return to the sea,
And no silver coat means she cannot swim free.
Sigrid is hungry and needs food in her tum,
Now the three are worried, because they have none!

The fish farm is near with juicy salmon fish,
So just wait for a seagull to drop his prime dish.

So, it's not long to wait as the seagull flies by,
And the fish that is caught, falls down from the sky.

Sigurd snatches the salmon and brings it to Drew,
Who serves it with seaweed and fat limpets too.

Sigrid's tum is now full
so she turns to the cave,
They all wave goodbye
and say,
"Keep being brave."

That mystery was solved in a **Blink** of an eye,
Then Drew laughed loudly!

What a silly Shrew am i!

YIPPPPEEEE!

OH NO!

Now time had passed too quickly and they all said their cheerful goodbyes!

They both ran towards the magic well, and jumped up very high.

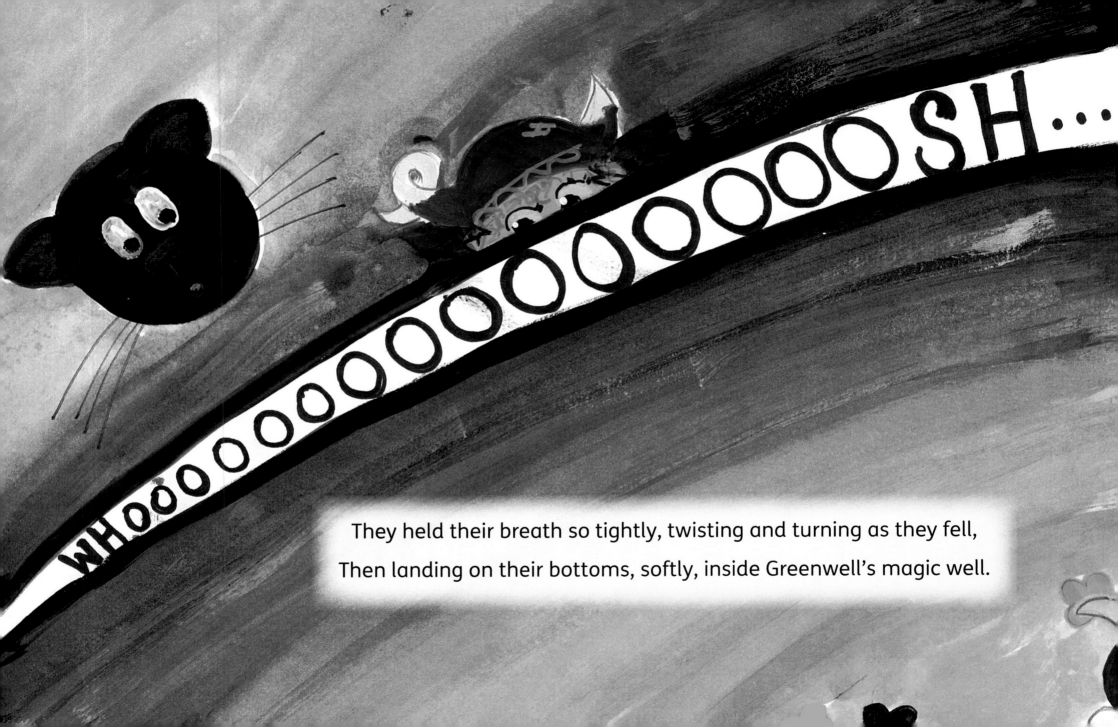

WHOOOOOOOOOOOOOOOOOOSH...

They held their breath so tightly, twisting and turning as they fell,

Then landing on their bottoms, softly, inside Greenwell's magic well.

A trill, a meow, a hug or two, but now comes morning light,

A really exciting adventure, they'd both had this very night.

But now it's time to go and check, on Farmer Ed and Jo . . .

The End

Beyla's message to you all.

Always try to be a good listener.

Listening is at the heart of a great friendship!

Know the difference between right and wrong and make sure that we try,

To always be kind to each other, and **never, ever lie**!

To make mistakes is part of life that helps us learn and grow,

To try our best in everything, as we journey on life's rainbow!

"No act of kindness, no matter how small, is ever wasted." (Aesop)

And tip-paw quietly back in the house, so all may never know.

HROO!
(That's **Hi** in Smoozle)

I'm Beyla and I just wanted to say to all my lovely readers this
VERY, VERY IMPORTANT MESSAGE.

PLEASE NEVER, EVER, EVER, EVER PLAY NEAR WATER ALONE.
ALWAYS HAVE AN ADULT BY YOUR SIDE.

I, BEYLA SMOOZLE HAVE MAGICAL POWERS
THAT HOOMANS DO NOT HAVE!

PLEASE NEVER, EVER, EVER, EVER JUMP INTO A WELL

IT IS VERY DANGEROUS

HREYE!
(That's **Thank you** in Smoozle)

Tiddles and me

Beyla Smoozle

These are
the
characters
in BOOK
THREE

Farmer Jo and
Jolly farmer Ed

Chuckziewoo and Teddybear

Tiddles the cat

aanus mouse

Drew

Sigurd